LIGHT ME UP

C.H. WILLIAMS

WEST 44 BOOKS™

Cataloging-in-Publication Data
Names: Williams, C.H.
Title: Light me up / C.H. Williams.
Description: Buffalo, NY : West 44, 2027. | Series: West 44 YA verse
Identifiers: ISBN 9781978598621 (pbk.) | ISBN 9781978598614 (library bound) | ISBN 9781978598638 (ebook)
Subjects: LCSH: High school students--Fiction. | Burns and scalds--Patients--Fiction. | Hospital patients--Fiction. | Friendship--Fiction.
Classification: LCC PZ7.1.W555 Li 2027 | DDC [F]--dc23

First Edition

Published in 2027 by
Enslow Publishing
2544 Clinton Street
Buffalo, NY 14224

Editor: Caitie McAneney
Designer: Tanya Dellaccio Keeney

Photo Credits: Cover (lightening texture) Thammanoon Khamchalee/Shutterstock.com.

Printed in the United States of America

CPSIA compliance information: Batch #CS27W44: For further information contact Enslow Publishing LLC at 1-800-398-2504.

For my two favorite humans

TEARS AND RAIN

track my cheeks.

I am soaked through,
and can no longer tell apart

the water from the storm
and the water from me.

I can't even take shelter
from this pouring rain

because I was taught
when there's lightning,

don't stand under a tree.

AND I CAN SEE THEM

but they can't see me.

I'm on the outside,
cloaked in night.

My only light
comes from the flashes above.
Like the lights from their phones

as they continue to dance
and laugh
and party

in my house
without me.

SEVEN HOURS EARLIER

I'M ON FIRE

or at least
that's what it feels like.

I sit in the classroom
as sweat pools in my bra.

My punk rock band tee
clings to me
like lyrics you can't forget.

My black hair
sticks to my forehead.

And when I scoop
it back into a ponytail,

my last elastic
br-e a-ks.

I want to SCREAM.

Shave.
My.
Head.

THE LUNCH BELL RINGS

and I unstick myself
from my seat.

Leaving behind
the imprint
of my thighs.

I bolt for the door
before anyone can
bar my way.

"There goes the rhino!"

Someone laughs.
Probably Eve.

"Bye, Jordan!"
someone calls all
fake nice.

Someone else shouts,
"Charge!"

I let the door
swing shut
behind me.

I SIT OUTSIDE

melting in my black jeans.

I curse the Florida sun.

And my dad
for dying,

just like that,
without even giving us
a heads-up.

One day here,
the next—
heart attack.

He left me here
all alone
with Mom.

I WORE YELLOW AT HIS FUNERAL

Everyone did.

He loved sunflowers
and surfing.

Tattoos
and piercings.

We would fly down
the highway
blasting old punk rock.

Dead Kennedys.
The Vandals.
Bad Religion.
Black Flag.

Then we'd park,
and he'd step out first,
coming around to
open my door.

DAD LOOKED LIKE A BULLDOG

He was hard as nails.
But he called me his sunshine.

And when he hugged me,
I never felt safer.

People had a hard time
understanding him too.

He didn't act
like the guy
people expected him
to be.

The big guy
    who surfed.

The tattooed punk
    who brought home flowers
    just because.

The best dad in the whole world
    who married . . . my mom.

BACK IN CLASS

we fan ourselves with
our notebooks.

The windows are open,
but there's no breeze.

There's no AC.

We sit and cook
in our seats.

It's so hot,
even the popular girls
sweat.

Beads of moisture
glisten on their
exposed skin.

The popular boys
eye them,
mouths gaping.

NO ONE

gapes at me
like that.

AND WHY WOULD THEY?

I'm no Eve.

Eve has olive skin,
full lips, hips, and thighs.
But an impossibly small waist.

I swear she defies science.

Sophia is the definition
of sun-kissed. Glowing.
The perfect spray of freckles.
Perfect waves in her chestnut hair.

Jessie, with her rich brown skin,
and bleached afro shaved close,
looks like she's stepped out
of a magazine.

Then there's Lily—
willowy and tall,
with long blond hair
without a single split end.

THEY'RE ALL SO DIFFERENT

Yet all so beautiful.

And then there's me.

My pale skin
reddens in the sun,
but I never glow.

My curves don't fit the same.
I don't have that hourglass frame.

My hair isn't pretty, fair,
or model chic.

It's mid-length
and dyed black.

Except for my roots,
which are a dull brown.

MR. MARSHALL

doesn’t care if you can’t
see the board
because your mom doesn’t let you
wear your glasses
to school.

If you need to sit closer
to hear him speak.

If you need to avoid
your bullies,

who spend his lessons
attacking the back

of your skull
with spitballs

or lacing your chair
with tacks.

No, Mr. Marshall
doesn’t care about
any of that.

I TRY TO FOCUS

on the assigned
reading.

But the text shifts
and sways
on the page.

My mind follows
my gaze

and drifts . . .

"Where can we go?"

Their voices are low
as they plot and plan
and scheme.

"Mom drained ours.
Hasn't refilled it yet."

JESSIE SIGHS

"Oh," Eve laughs.
"It's not because
of the drought."

I lean back a touch

to listen in.

"She's all weird about germs.
She gets them to empty
the pool

then refill it, like,
once a month."

"BEACH?"

Sophia's suggestion
is met with a groan.

"No, thanks." Eve snorts.

"Salt water doesn't work
with this hair."

I stifle a laugh,
but I'm not quick enough.

Someone taps my shoulder,
and I cautiously turn.

"What's so funny?" Eve asks.

Her cronies scowl,
on either side.

Backing her up.

I WINCE

"Nothing."

This would be a great time
for Mr. Marshall to tell
me to face the front.

No such luck.

EVE CRACKS A SMILE

"Hey. You have a pool,
right?"

I swallow,
but the air in here is so dry.

I blink,
and shrink
in my seat.

Nod, Jordan.
Do something.
Say something!

Anything.
Please!

"Yes?" I say finally.

THEY FACE EACH OTHER

They grin.

"Can we use it?"
Eve asks.

Except she never asks.
She takes.

"Jordan. Eyes on the board."
Mr. Marshall calls.

Too late.

"Yeah. Um. Sorry."
I turn back.

But then Eve leans in.

"So? Can we?"

She whispers
directly
into my ear.

I shiver
despite the heat.

SHE STAYS

until I nod.

Only then
does she sit back.

Her breath gone.

WHEN CLASS LETS OUT

they surround me like
roses around a post.

All beauty and smiles,
but thorny at the same time.

I bend to their will.

Though it should be
the other way
around.

"So, it'll just be you guys
coming over?"

They shrug and smile.

"Because my mom's working tonight
and—"

Eve's eyes light up.
"And your dad?"

I look down.
"He's . . ."

It's been six months,
but I still can't bring myself to say it.

"He's not around."

EVE RAISES ONE BROW

"No brothers or sisters?" she asks.

I shake my head.

"We'll have the place
to ourselves."

"Nice." Eve grins.

"Yeah, cool," Sophia adds.

Then Lily,
the quiet one,
says,
"Thank you."

And it's nice to hear
at least one of them
say it.

EVE SNATCHES LILY'S PHONE

then gives it
to me.

I stare at it blankly.

"We need your address."

Jessie smirks.
Eve sighs then taps the screen.

She opens the Notes App,
then hands it back.

"We haven't got all day."

I type it in.
"See you later then?"

Eve bats her lashes.

"And if you could like,
get us some snacks?"

I NOD

"No problem."

They walk away,
and I let out a long breath.

They're coming over
to MY house.
To use MY pool.
To hang out with ME.

I allow myself
a tiny smile.

This is it.
My chance to make friends.

To finally,
FINALLY
fit in.

I RAID THE STORE

on my way home.

Getting

ALL OF THE SNACKS

I pile cookies
and chips
and candy
in my arms.

As much as I can carry.
I'll fill my schoolbag.

(I don't have a car.)

The checkout lady
scowls as she scans.

Giving me that look,
like, *This all for you?*

I grin back
at her silent question.

"I'm having friends over."

Her eyebrows rise
with surprise—
or disbelief.

OUR HOUSE

isn’t big

or showy
or special.

But we have a pool,
which is what they asked for.

So there’s that.

I walk through the overgrown grass
to the front door.

There was a time
where I could have gone
straight around the back.

But now the weeds
are so overgrown
they fill the gaps

between the house
and the fence on either side.

They press in on our house.

They are impossibly dry
because of this heat wave.

DAD USED TO KEEP

our yard all neat and tidy,
with his push mower.

Mom doesn't mow.

Sure, she's all about appearances . . .
except when it comes to our home.

Well, it was always Dad's job.
His other job.
On top of his regular job, I mean.

He was a tattoo artist,
so he worked odd hours

and was able to book his clients
around other things,

like school pickup times
and parent evenings.

BUT HE ALWAYS MADE TIME

for the other things:

like keeping up with
the house,
the yard,

and me.

When he died,
I guess I thought Mom
would take over.

I hoped she'd step up.

But her corporate job
has always come before
the house,
the yard,

and me.

I LIFT MY KEY TO THE DOOR

but pause when I hear
a truck behind me.

I whirl around.

Someone’s reversing a huge van
into our neighbors’ driveway.

They park at an angle,
and I peer at the side.

It’s a moving van.

My gaze hitches on the
space where this morning there
was still a FOR SALE sign.

A MAN GETS OUT

then jogs around

to open the door
on the driver's side.

A woman takes his hand
then steps on to the driveway.

They kiss,
and I avert my gaze.

Jeez. I get it.
You're in love.

I frown.
Mom said she and Dad
were like that too, once upon a time.

Before they had me.

Which means . . .
these two probably don't have kids.

OR MAYBE THEY DO . . .

This lanky teen
—my age?—
hops down next.

I turn away.

I swear the second I get inside,
I am putting my glasses on.

I couldn't even see
that there were three people

sitting in the cab up front.

I turn the key,
but before I head in

I glance back.

The boy waves

at me.

STUNNED,

I wave back.

Then quickly go in.

I drop my bag.

Snacks spill out
over the tiled floor.

Argh!

I can't do this!

What was I thinking??

I MOP AND CLEAN AND SCRUB

what I can.

But whatever I do,
it doesn't feel like enough.

The pool calls to me,
as it did to them.

The heat makes me weak
to the cool water,

and I think about
diving in.

But I can't.
Not yet.

First,
I have to make friends.

TONIGHT

I'll be the cool girl.
The pool girl.

Not the weirdo punk kid
sweating in all black
at the back
of the class.

Squinting at the board
because Mom says
my glasses make my face
look fat.

She's even worse now Dad's gone.

You're just like him,
she says, but never in a nice way.
He just LOVED to eat.
And you can see how
that ended.

Like I need reminding.

Mom would rather I was
skinny and blind.

NOW, OF COURSE

she claims to simply,
want better for my health,
because of what happened to Dad . . .

But what about before?

What about when I was
a skinny seven-year-old

being told to portion my carbs
to the size of my tiny fist?

At the time,
none of my friends
even knew what carbs were.

Bet their moms never
checked if they could touch
their thumb and middle finger
around their wrist.

I LAY OUT THE SNACKS

Chuck my phone on charge
just in case.

Then force myself to leave
the kitchen.

I get hungry when I'm nervous.

When the time comes, I stand by the open
door.

Does it make me look too eager?
I retreat.

I close the door.
Will they know I'm here?

I open it again,
then go back to the kitchen.

I eat just one thing from each of the plates.
There's plenty left.

THEY BARELY EAT ANYWAY

"Hello?"

I swallow my mouthful,
and am halfway to the sink
with the empty plate
when Eve strolls in.

She wears a tiny two-piece swimsuit
and a smirk.

"There you are!"

Her gaze travels from my face
to the empty plate in my hands.

She cocks her head to one side,
then tuts.

"You didn't start without us,
did you?"

troop in before I can reply.

They're all laughter and chitchat.
Inside jokes and gossip.

Lily follows
quietly behind.

She waves when she sees me,
and I wave back.

"H-Help yourself to—"

I gesture to the spread of snacks,
then reach across to adjust two bowls
to fill the empty space
I just made.

EVE SCOWLS

"I'm intolerant."

I bite back an awkward laugh.

Jessie rolls her eyes.
"She's low-carb."

Eve huffs. "I'm gluten free."

I look down.
"I'm sorry. I didn't know,
or I would have—"

Sophia grabs a piece of candy,
then stares me down,
mouth open as she chews.

"You should have asked."

I SHOW THEM TO THE POOL

When the doorbell rings,
I double back.

Who could that be?

It's Tim . . . or maybe Tom?
He's from our school,
but I don't think we share
any classes.

"Sup." He raises his chin,
then walks past me.

I step back,
then turn to watch him.

"Er . . . Do you—"

He's not listening.

I RETURN TO THE POOL

Eve sits on the side,
her long legs over the edge.
She dips her toes in the water.

Jessie and Sophia splash and squeal and swim.

Lily's lower body is submerged,
her arms crisscrossed on the edge,
as she smiles up at me.

I look around.
Stunned to find

Tim or Tom
taking off his shirt,

before he
dives
right
in.

EVE POINTS AND LAUGHS

as he surfaces,
jolting his head
to sweep his wet hair from his face.

"You're such a dork!" she tells him
with a broad smile.

When she says it to him,
it sounds like a good thing.

He swims over to her,
then grabs her legs.
She shrieks and bats him away.

Then they stop
and turn to face me.

They both grin wide
and wave.

I CAN'T BELIEVE IT

They're finally waving to me!

I make my way over.

This is it.

I stride toward them.

They're inviting me to join in!

"You made it!" Eve's eyes shine with glee.

I pause.

"I . . . what?"

TIM OR TOM PUSHES UP

and out of the pool.

He moves toward me,
still smiling,
then he skirts to one side.

He passes me,
without looking.

Like I'm not even a person

but a fire hydrant
or a tree
or an old couch
on the street.

Obstructing the sidewalk.

In the way
but not person enough to
warrant an "Excuse me."

I WHIRL AROUND

They weren't waving
at me.

Three more classmates show up.
Then another four.
Another five.

Heart racing,
I turn on my heel.
Rush back inside.

I go to close my front door,
but more people walk in.
Walk past me,
just like Tim or Tom did.

Like I'm not even standing here,
breathing and alive.

I hear music.
But it's not mine.

I GO TO THE KITCHEN

to catch my breath.

To grab a bite.
To comfort myself.
To work out what my plan is now.

I open the kitchen door,
and half the snacks are gone.

There are people everywhere.
Some I don't even vaguely recognize.

"Heads up!" one shouts,
then launches a . . . beer can? . . .
over my head.

I DUCK

The guy behind me
pops a tab.

Ker-chushhh.

The beer sprays my back
and he laughs as I turn,
jolting away
from the frothing, fizzing can
in his outstretched hand.

It's in my hair.
It's on my shirt,
my jeans.

It's all over me!

Tears spring to my eyes
as I storm out.

"What?"
More laughter, then—
"She could use a shower anyway!"

I WEAVE THROUGH BODIES

Pushing past dozens of people.
It's a mess.
It's a rave.

People dance to the blaring bass
of the music pumping through
the two huge speakers
someone has placed on my living room floor.

I can't hear.
I can't handle this.
I can't think straight.

MORE PEOPLE POUR IN

and there's no space to breathe.

It's so hot.
I thought outside was bad.
But it's truly like an oven in here.

I'm being buried alive by the press
of my classmates,
only half of whom I can name.

It's humid,
and I'm soaked.
Sticky with someone else's beer.

My vision blurs
as tears fill my eyes,
and I can barely make it
from here to the other side

of my house.

BUT I GET THERE

I reach the stairs,
then sit on the bottom step,
and take a second to breathe.

I start to count to 10,
but I can hardly hear the numbers
in my head.

One . . .

Two . . .

Three . . .

Thunder booms above,
or perhaps it's the thumping bass?

I cover my ears with my hands.

I should call the police.
Call the whole thing off.

BUT THEN AGAIN . . .

If I let this happen.
If I can just let this go.
If I can be cool and chill and fun . . .

Maybe I'll make some friends?
Have something to *do* after school?
Not be so alone?

Tonight—

> I'm not Jordan,
> the rhino,
> the punk,
> the fat girl with no friends.

It's MY house.
This is MY party.

Dad always said,
> "You'll find your people."

I look down . . .
> because he also said, "Just be yourself."

MY PEOPLE

must be here somewhere . . .

I stand.

I just have to find them.

THUNDER BOOMS AGAIN

And lightning strikes in the distance.

Perfect.

After all,
as the host of this party,
it's my duty to look after my guests.

I'll simply tell Eve and the others
they have to come inside—
for safety.

Then maybe I'll find a song
they like (and I don't totally despise),

and we can sing
and dance.

We can hang out

like we planned?

WHEN THEY SEE

how unbothered I am
by the chaos and the mess.

When they see how
cool and chill and relaxed
I can be with a house full of strangers—

they'll marvel at me.

They'll think, *Actually, Jordan's not so bad!*
They'll think, *She's actually pretty cool.*
They'll see me how Dad saw me . . .

as someone who's happy
and kind
and fun to be around.

I STRIDE THROUGH THE MASSES

(way too many people to count!)

I head for the back door,
then open it wide.

More thunder.
More lightning.

I shout to be heard
over the music behind me.
"The storm's getting pretty bad!"

They look over,
then shrug.

I walk right up to the pool's edge.

"You should come in," I beckon.
"We've um . . . got towels."

DUH

I wince.
Why would I even say that?

"We've also got . . . beer," I add.

Eve's eyebrows rise.

Then like a sprinkler
being turned on,
the rain starts
and they retreat.

And sure,
it would have been nice
if they had come in
because I had asked.

But, nevermind.

I sigh, turning to follow them.

EVE HALTS AT THE DOOR

"Wait! My phone!" she gasps.

The others carry on inside,
leaving just me and her.

Eve points past me and
I look back over my shoulder.

I don't see it,
but then again—

I can't see much.

"It's over there." She faces me.
"Can you grab it?"

I nod.
"Of course!"

The rain's heavier now.

THE MUSIC IS MUTED

as I return poolside.

I retrace my steps,
retracing hers,

but I can’t see her phone anywhere.

I can hardly see my hand
in front of my face
with all this rain
and without my glasses.

The sky lights up,
and thunder roars overhead
making me jump.

But I can’t give up.

I’ll find it for her,
and she’ll be so happy!

Then we’ll all hang out.

WHERE IS IT?

Where is it?!

I desperately scan the poolside.
I scan the pool itself.

I look back,
but it's all a blur,

and the door is closed.
They must be waiting for me inside.

Eve is trusting me with this.
She's counting on me.

IT'S NO USE!

I shake my head,
rushing back.

If I stay out here any longer
without finding it,
it'll get ruined in the rain!

"I'm so sorry!" I yell,
as I lumber back through the yard.

I reach the door. "I—"

Eve, all alone,
holds her phone
up to the glass.

I grin. *Thank god!*

I reach for the door handle,
but—

THE DOOR'S LOCKED

I shake my head.
"Let me in!" I laugh.

Eve steps back,
cupping a hand around her ear.

"What?" she mouths.

I point to the door handle.
"It's locked!" I call louder.

Eve shrugs.
Her smile drops.

She turns away, and—

WAIT

I rap on the door.

"Eve!"

I call out.

THUNDER.
LIGHTNING.
RAIN.

"Eve!" I shout again.

I pound harder,
my fists pale against the glass.

"Eve!" I'm shrill now.
"Let me in!"

But it's no use.
She's gone.

And she's the only one
who knows I'm still out here.

I TAKE A STEP BACK

Then another.
Then another.

And wow.

I mean. Just look.

If Dad had been here
to see how many people could fit

in our little house,
he would have laughed.

He would have grumbled
about their music choices,
but he would have cranked it louder anyway.

He would have left the doors
- open wide -

The more the merrier!

DAD NEVER *PLAYED* IT COOL

He just
was.

BOOM!

The thunder is so loud
it burrows inside my skull.

Filling the places
memories seeped in before.

I curse the rain
and the weeds
and my dad
and this day.

Then I break down.
I sob.

This is what I get
for trying to be more like him.

IT'S NOT FAIR

I check my pockets.

- Empty -

I left my phone inside!

I didn't think I'd need it.

I thought we'd be too busy
chatting,
swimming,
hanging out.

MORE THUNDER

** Lightning sparks **

I'm getting cold.
It's getting dark.

I shiver,
crying now.

Shaking with sobs.

The storm takes hold of me.

I'm wrapped in its embrace,
but as the rain pours,
and the thunder roars,
and the wind whips
my wet hair
into my face—

I SEE IT

The lightning.

- Everything slows -

Everything is silenced,
even the rain.

My ears ring,
yet I can't hear anything.

Until . . .

CRACK!

THE SPARKS TAKE

despite the rain,

and from them
come flames

that lick and lap
at the roof.

At MY roof.
At the roof of MY house.

My house is on fire . . .

Yet part of me still wants in.

LIGHTNING FORKS

It stabs
like a knife.

It can split trees.
It can set things alight.
It can burn a house.

Thunder laughs and claps
at the show beneath it.

Then like a sitting duck,
I become its next target.

It strikes and all I feel is:

*

*

*

WHITE

*

*

*

HOT

*

*

*

HEAT

*

*

*

*

I CLOSE MY EYES

It hurts.

Make it stop.

Let me burn.

THEN—

A savior.

"Dad?" Tears sting my eyes.
"Is it really you?"

His smile is a break in the clouds.

He puts a hand on my shoulder,
his touch so gentle,
I can hardly feel it.

"You hang in there,
sunshine."

I BLINK. EYES WIDE.

“She’s awake.”

I sit up,
or at least I try to . . .

I groan as the room around me
swims into view.

I will my body
to do as it’s told.

I’m a heavy girl,
but I’ve never been *this* heavy.

My bones are lead beneath my skin.
I can’t even lift my arms.

I BLINK

and blink.

But I'm awake already.

And I'm dry.
I must have made it inside!

But the thumping bass
has been replaced
by intermittent beeps . . .

Beep.

Beep.

Be-Beep!

Beep.

Is that me?

I squint at my arm.

My band tee gone . . .

There's tape and . . . a tube?

AND BANDAGES

Oh God.

I heave.

There's a needle sticking out of me!

The beeps go berserk
as I flail around.

I taste iron.

I smell . . . disinfectant,
chemicals,
cleaning solution,

but also . . . burnt flesh.

I think I'm gonna hurl.

UNIFORMS RUSH IN

This is a hospital.
I'm in a hospital?

I'm all bandaged up.

No. No way.

I can't.

It can't be.

That smell of burning flesh . . .

I gag.

I think that smell
is coming from me.

I'M HEAVY AGAIN

Though this time
it's my eyes.

Words follow me
into the abyss.

"Call her mom.
Tell her she should come back in."

I WAKE AGAIN

And there she is.

Mom's in her usual office attire.
Her gray skirt suit screams
I work in finance!

I can never picture her
the way Dad said she was
when they met.

My tears brim
as her concerned gaze meets mine.

She rushes to me,
and I'm warm.

THEN HER FACE TURNS

thunderous.

“What the heck were you thinking?”

I grow cold
as she brings her face
close to mine.

“You stupid, stupid girl.” She seethes.
“You burned the whole house down.”

She backs up
as a nurse appears.

I blink back tears.

I burned the house down?
What?

But Mom’s right.
She’s always right.

Whatever happened,
it’s my fault.

HOURS PASS

I sleep.
I breathe.
I hurt.
I make it through the night.

Where'd Mom go?

Did she just . . . leave me?

Nurses feed and water me
like a plant.

They see to the burn on my shoulder.
They call it "the entry point."

They change my bandages
(which stink by the way).

And I'm told over and over
how lucky I am.

THEY MOVE ME

to the small pediatric burns unit,
and I'm left alone,
until . . .

They draw the curtain around
and someone moves
into the bay next door.

"This is Vinny Owens.
Fifteen years old."

I hold my breath.

"Second-degree burns on the arms and back,
approximately 20 percent total body surface area."

That seems like a lot.

"Smoke inhalation
with moderate respiratory distress."

He was in a fire.

I don't catch the rest . . .

AND I KNOW IT'S SELFISH

but I'm kinda relieved.

Maybe now I'll have someone
to talk to?

Mom hasn't been back.

And I only see Dad
in my dreams.

I listen
from my side of the curtain.

I listen hard
          all day long.

But I'm too shy to speak.

HIS PARENTS VISIT

and they are SO NICE.

It's almost painful
to have them just on the other side
of the curtain.

Giving so much love,
and being so so kind.

When my own mother
can hardly look at me.

It's late when they leave.
I wish they could have stayed longer.

Not for him,
but for me.

I'M DWELLING ON THIS

when I hear—

[Hello.]

I look around.

That wasn't a regular voice.
It almost sounded like it
came from—

a robot?

I shake my head.
They must have upped my meds.

[I'm just trying something here.]

I freeze.

[Can you hear me?]

It's coming from the next bay over.

FROM THE BURNED BOY

Vinny.

"Um . . . yeah? I can hear you."

[She talks.] the robot voice states.

My eyebrows knit together.
"Why do you sound like that?"

[I'm on vocal rest.]

"Huh?"

He falls silent for a moment, then—
[It's a text-to-speech app.]

Ohhh . . .

[I just downloaded it on my phone.]

Okay?

[Are you still there?]

"Yes." I roll my eyes.

WHERE ELSE WOULD I BE?

[I'm Vinny.]

I shrug. "I'm Jordan."

[I know.]

I frown.

I mean, sure,
I've heard the staff
and his parents talking about him.

Makes sense he'd have
heard them talking about me.

"Then why'd you ask?"

[This is how you make conversation,
Jordan.]

I pout.
"I know how to make conversation!"

[Easy now.]

I SCOWL

"Well, this is not making me
want to talk to you!"

[Sure it is.]

My eyebrows rise.
"Is not."

I sound so childish.

[But it is working.]
[Isn't it?]
[Jordan.]

I'd cross my arms if they weren't
so bandaged and burned.

"No."

I sigh. Yes.

[It's nice to meet you.]

I LAUGH

despite myself
for the first time in . . .

            How long has it been?

[Made you laugh.]

I roll my eyes some more.

“Fine. You got me.”
Am I actually smiling?

[Yay.]

FINE. I'LL PLAY ALONG

"I guess it's nice to meet you too."

[Heard you got struck by lightning.]

"Um yeah . . . I guess I did."

[You guess?]

I pout.

"Okay. Yes. I got struck by lightning."
Wow. That's the first time
I've said it out loud.

[So when you said,
you guess it's nice to meet me . . .]

I shake my head smiling.
That's his follow up question?

Really?

[I'm flattered.]

I shake my head some more.

"Whatever."

[ANY SUPERPOWERS?]

My eyebrows draw close.
"Huh?"

[Did you get superpowers?]
[You know. From the bolt?]

I chuckle.
It hurts.

"Um . . . not that I know of?"

[Not yet, you mean.]

My cheeks heat.
Am I blushing?

"I could be superfast.
Only I can't get out of bed."

[Or super strong?]

I shake my head.
"I'm not strong."

MY WORDS COME OUT QUIET

I didn't mean
to say that.

Since I woke up,
I've been feeling heavy,

not just in my body,
but in my mind.

Heavy with guilt.
Heavy with pain
and self-pity.

Heavy with anger.
Heavy with worry.
Heavy with loss.
Heavy with . . .

isolation.

BUT NOW . . .

[I ran into a burning building.]

I nod. Go figure.

"So you're already a superhero."

[Or really, really dumb.]

I small laugh escapes me.

"Reckless maybe.
          But not dumb."

Whereas what I did . . .

I swallow.

You stupid, stupid girl.

Tears well as Mom's words
echo in my mind.

You burned the whole house down.

THEN HE TYPES . . .

[I'm a rebel. Reckless.]
[Running headfirst.]
[Reckless.]
[You hate us cause we're restless.]

I gape at the curtain,
and the boy hidden behind it.

No.
He didn't . . .

He couldn't?

I replay his words in my head.

"I'm a rebel. Reckless.
Running headfirst. Reckless.
You hate us cause we're restless . . ."

Out loud,
I finish the lyrics:

"You hate us cause we're reckless."

HE TYPES FASTER

[Hold up.]
[You know Frenzy State?]

I gasp.
"Do I *know* them?"

The monitor beeps as my heart rate rises.

"I'm OBSESSED with them."

[I don't believe you.]

I gape some more.
"I don't believe *you*!"

[You *googled* the lyrics.]

"I don't even have my phone."

[For real?]

HIS MONITORS BEEP WILDLY TOO

"For real!"

[You might just be the coolest girl I've ever met.]

I beam. "I guess so."

[You guess correct.]

THE CURTAIN AROUND MY BAY FLIES OPEN

A nurse marches over.

Footsteps sound on
Vinny's side too.

My nurse fusses over me,
checking this and that.

She looks me over,
taking notes.

And I . . .

I can't help it.
I get the giggles.

She pauses, her pen raised.
"What's gotten into you?"

The nurse next door
seems to be asking Vinny the same.

I PICTURE A SMILE

mirroring my own.

Only his face is a blur,
like he's just out of range.

But I can hear him smiling
from the other side of the curtain.

I swear I can.

BUT THEN—

“Put that phone away,” his nurse says.
“You need your rest!”

“I’m sorry,” I say, immediately.
“It was my fault.
I wound him up!”

My nurse gives me one last
disapproving stare.

“If this hospital had a larger burn unit,
I’d separate you two.”

And we don’t dare
say anything else,
until they’re both long gone.

Once I’m sure we’re alone

—or as alone as we can be
in this place—

I open my mouth to speak.

BUT VINNY GETS THERE FIRST

[Not very Frenzy State of you.]
[Apologizing like that.]

I look down, grinning.
“I guess I’m not much of a rebel.”

[Nah. I bet you’re plenty reckless.]

I’m definitely blushing.

“Don’t get me all riled up again.
What if they take away your phone?”

Can they even do that?

He’s quiet a moment,
and I realize,

if they take his phone,
they take his voice.

I DON'T WANT TO BE ALONE AGAIN

[Talk tomorrow?]

And I'm grinning again.
Looking forward to it already.

"Okay."

Then for good measure, I add:

"It'd be reckless
to keep talking tonight."

I'M DROWSY

when the nurses come
around for their morning checks.

I feel dopey
from all the medication.

I wince when they change my bandages
though I try my best
not to make a fuss.

Not **out loud** at least.

I'm sure my discomfort
shows on my face well enough.

Vinny doesn't talk.
Maybe he's asleep.
Maybe they took his phone.

OR MAYBE I MADE HIM UP?

Maybe I was so lonely,
I conjured a friend.

Someone who loves
my favorite band.

I mean,
how could he possibly know
Frenzy State?

When I saw them in concert,
they weren't even the main event.

They were the support band.
The warm-up band!

I wasn't even supposed
to be at that gig!

I was too young to get in.

But of course,
my dad charmed
the doormen.

THEIR LEAD SINGER IS A GIRL

She has jet-black hair
in a mullet,
a mess of curls.

When she sang live,
it made *me* feel powerful.

Dad bought me a band tee
from their tiny merch stall.

I wore it right away.

When we got home,
I downloaded all their albums
on my phone.

And now it's all gone,
I suppose.

My phone.
That T-shirt.
The very last parts of Dad
I still own.

[GOOD MORNING.]

The clock reads 2 p.m.

I try to settle
the soaring butterflies
in my stomach.

"I thought maybe you'd died."
I deadpan, trying to be funny.

[Nah. That would be rude.]

I scoff. "Rude?"

[Yeah. Rude.]

I shake my head. "How?"

[Well, I can't go dying in my sleep
after saying I'll talk tomorrow.]

He remembered.

HE'S REAL

[Anyway.]
[Do you think it's too early for music?]

I shift in my bed,
then grimace with pain.

"Guess it depends what type of music."

[There you go, guessing again.]

I look down.
I didn't realize how much I do that.

Guessing.

[I want to play you a song.]

I light up. "Yeah?"

[Lemme find it. One sec.]

I WAIT WITH BATED BREATH

Guitar.
Gritty.
Urgent.
Distorted.

Then the singing
starts—

His words,
his lyrics,
come out angry and fast.

I press the button
on the side of my bed
so I can sit up straighter,
so I can listen harder.

Then a girl takes the mic.
And I swear I'd have goosebumps
if I had any unburned skin left
on my arms.

SHE'S NOT GRUFF

like the girl from Frenzy State.
But there's something in her voice
that makes me ache
to see a live band again.

I close my eyes,
then picture them on stage.

The pace quickens,
and they alternate verses.

He's shouting,
and she's singing back to him,
like it's a battle
of the genres.

Then the guitars cut out,
and the drumming stops.

Cymbals discarded.

Their voices blend
as he sings
and she shouts
at the end.

IN THE SILENCE THAT FOLLOWS

I ask breathlessly, "What was that?"

[The No Good Ones.]

Never heard of them.

[My band.]

"*Your* band?"
I blink at the curtain between us.

[Yep.]

I have no words.

[I'm kinda hoping
all the smoke I took in
will make me sound even better
in the long run.]

The smoke.
The house fire.
Vocal rest.

I can't believe he could
sing like that.

But what if . . .

NOW . . .

He might never sing again.

I PLEAD

"Play another one!"

[As you wish.]

This one starts with a crash
of cymbals.

It's high energy.
Fast-paced.

I close my eyes.
It's like Dad's here with me again.

No one ever likes
music like this.

It was my thing.
Mine and Dad's.

But now—

THE MUSIC STOPS

"This is a hospital."

Must be one of the nurses.

"What were you thinking?"

A curtain draws back
as she mutters under her breath.

"Honestly. Kids these days."

I can't help but laugh.
I hope somehow he's laughing with me.

"Brutal," I tell him.

[You didn't apologize this time.]

I smirk. "And I never will again."

VINNY'S PARENTS VISIT AGAIN

They were here just yesterday.

I didn't know they were allowed
to visit that often.

Vinny sleeps through the afternoon.

Yet they still come
to sit with him.

His mom even sings.
Quietly.
Respectfully.

So unlike the punk songs
that he sings and I listen to.

I picture her stroking his hair—
if he has any left.

I don't know what he looked
like before,

all I know is the percentage
of his skin that is now burned.

ONCE THEY'RE GONE

I get him all to myself.

We talk as if we've known each other
for a lifetime,

but also like we're desperately
trying to catch each other up.

We talk all night.

I've never had a friend like this:

someone my age
who likes the same stuff.

AND IT'S NOT JUST MUSIC

Though I still can't get over that.

We like the same movies,
the same TV shows.

And when he tells me
he wants to learn
how to surf one day,

I tell him, "I'll teach you."

and he types: [Okay. Bet.]

I FALL ASLEEP SMILING

We talked so much
his phone is now dying.

But it doesn't matter
how sweetly I fall asleep.

The night terrors
wait for me.

I lie there sweating,
unable to forget

how I stood there
rooted to the spot.

The lights went out.
The music stopped.

I WAKE IN A POOL OF SWEAT

My heart pounds.

"I can't get in," I sob
as the dim light of the ward
pulls me back to the present.

Blearily, I look around.
It was just a bad dream.

[Jordan?]

"I'm okay," I tell him.
Just totally embarrassed.

[I'm here.]

I shake my head
and rub my eyes.

A PAUSE

I hear the clicks
as he types.
Stops.
Types again.

[You're safe now.]

I nod, tears still streaming
down my face.

[I'm here if you wanna talk about it.]

My voice is all watery,
but I manage to reply, "Thanks."
I swallow. "I'm . . . I'm okay."

[If you change your mind,
you know where I am.]

Right here next to me.

WE FALL SILENT

Our human noises
grow quiet.

The machines
beep and hum
and breathe.

It's crazy how I
haven't heard Vinny
speak.

I'm so used to his
tinny robot voice now,

I forget it's not
actually him.

I've only ever
heard him sing . . .

I've only ever heard
the punk version of him.

IT'S 4 A.M.

The lights are always on.
Someone's always home.

The nurses make their rounds
day and night
and day again.

Someone's always *on call.*

And I can't get back to sleep.

I LOOK OVER AT THE CURTAIN

I wish I could see his face.

“Vinny?” I whisper.
“Are you awake?”

I wait.
And I wait.

Then—

[What’s up, little rebel?]

I grin.

“Just thinking . . .”

[About what?]
[About me?]

“Oh, ha ha.”

I HEAR HIM SMILING AGAIN

"It's just . . .
Do you ever wish
you could go back?"

I mean, of course he does.
No one wants to be here.

Except . . .

[Yes and no.]

My eyebrows rise.
"You don't just want to,
y'know . . . press *undo*?"

Wish *I* could.
But then again . . .

[I'm in a lot of pain.
My throat is wrecked.
I might never sing again.
But . . .]

"But?"

[If I wasn't here,
I wouldn't have met you.]

I BITE MY LIP

I was thinking the same.

"I dunno. Maybe we would have still met
somewhere, someday."

[Maybe.]

"I mean, maybe I would have
seen you at a show . . ."

[Maybe you would have
come to one of our gigs.]

"Maybe." I smile.
"I guess we'll never know."

[You're guessing again.]

"Oh, quiet you."

HE STOPS TYPING

"Just kidding."

[I know.]

[Would you go back?]
[Would you press undo?]

I LOOK DOWN

at my bandaged arms.

My dressings are white
with a blue hue
from the monitor's lights.

I no longer smell of burned flesh,
but it's also not like my arms
will ever look the same again.

Turns out turning a little rosy in the sun
is nothing compared to this.

[So?]

I GIVE IN

"Yes and no."

[Hey. That was my line.]

I chuckle quietly.
"Well, you made a good point."

[I did?]

"If I'd just done things differently . . ."

You stupid, stupid girl.

I shut my eyes, but her words
are burned into my mind.

She hasn't even come back
to remind me.

It's been . . .

three days?

TEARS WELL

and I can't help it.

"If I hadn't . . ."

I don't want any of this.
I don't want my mom to hate me.

I don't even want to be friends
with Sophia and Lily.
With Jessie or Eve.

Being here with Vinny
makes me question
what we would have even
talked about.

They hate my music.
They hated the snacks I bought.
I'm pretty sure they hate me.

I WANT TO TAKE IT ALL BACK

Because it was a mistake.

I want to try again
and do better this time around.

I lift the sheet to wipe my eyes.

"But yeah . . .
Now I've got you so . . ."

[Maybe our friendship
is worth the pain.]

I DON'T KNOW

when we fall asleep.

I just assume at some point we do.

Because it's light in here now,
and I'm wide awake.

Vinny's parents visit.
His mom sings to him.
His dad prays.

Vinny doesn't say a single word
to me.

Or anyone else.

All day.

I LISTEN FROM MY BED

And he's still there.

The nurses do their rounds,
and I eavesdrop on his updates.

He's still there.
And he's doing okay.

HIS PARENTS LEAVE

and I hear tapping.

[Jordan. You there?]

I light up inside.

"Where else would I be?"

[My phone's been on charge
all day.]

[I did listen out for you.]

[But when I was awake,
I was pretty sure you were asleep.]

I wasn't.
But I don't tell him that.

"Can you ask your parents
to bring in a portable charger for you?"

WAS THAT A STUPID THING TO SAY?

[An excellent idea.]

I grin at the praise.

Then I sigh,
staring out at the far side of the room.

The view from the window
is a sky-blue blur.

I can't even get my mom
to bring in my glasses.

I haven't had a chance to ask.

SHE HASN'T BEEN HERE

[Hey Jordan.]

I smirk. "Hey Vinny."

[Mom's asking if you want
her to bring you anything?]

My heart lodges in my throat.

"Um . . ."

I shake my head.
"No. No, I'm okay."

[Lemme know if you change your mind.]
[You know what I miss the most?]

"What?" I ask, a little teary still.

[My mom's mac 'n' cheese.]
[I hate this stupid feeding tube.]

ASHAMED

I look down.

I've been drowning in self-pity.

My wounds are healing.
I've even regained some feeling.

Yet Vinny can't even eat.

THE ONLY THING

I'm really struggling with
. . . is sleep.

"You'll have to eat it first thing
when you get out," I say.

"I'm sure your mom will
spoil you rotten."

[Yeah.]
[She will.]

At least there's that.

[Could take a while though.]
[I don't know when
I'll be going home.]

I SCOWL

"At least you have a home."
There I go again.
Making everything about me.

[You don't have a home?]

Urgh. Why did I say that?

I'm so stupid.
Stupid, stupid girl.

"Not anymore."
I try to laugh it off.

It's not funny though.

[What happened?]

I don't want to burden him.
He's been through enough.

HE RAN INTO A HOUSE FIRE

And I all but created one.

Or at least, that's how it feels.

I can't control the weather,
but . . .

I could have said no.

I could have stayed in.
Alone.

I didn't have to let them in.
I didn't have to let it get
that bad.

And yeah,
lightning may have still struck the house.

But it might not have.
I'll never know.

I AVOID HIS QUESTION

asking one of my own.

“Why did you do it?
Why’d you run into that house?”

[I guess I was trying to be
a hero.]

I bite my lip.
“You guess?”

[Don’t start.]

I smile. “Okay. I won’t.”

I CAN HEAR HIM TYPING

Then—

[We just moved in
to our new house that day.]

His story lurches through the curtain
from his phone.

[We unpacked.]

[Then went out for food.
But when we got back . . .]

[The house across from us
was on fire.]

I SWALLOW

[There were EMTs,
and fire engines.]

[And a bunch of teens outside
watching it all light up.]

[Then this girl started yelling,
saying one of her friends
was still inside.]

[And I don't know what
got into me . . .]

[I just ran.]

I LISTEN TO HIS STORY

But it can't be the same.
It just can't be.

My stomach twists and knots.
I double over.
I can't breathe.

But no.
It doesn't make any sense.

If Vinny's my new neighbor,
then who was this *friend*?

I don't have anyone.

No one there would have cared,
or even noticed
I hadn't made it out.

Would they?

But if someone did . . .

THAT WOULD MEAN—

[I wanted to save her.]

I gasp but can't catch my breath.
I clutch my throat.

No!

My heart pounds.
"You ran into a burning building for . . .
for someone you didn't even know?"

[I never said I was smart . . .]

"Then what happened?" I ask,
my voice hushed.

[Well, I got in there
and the place was trashed.]

[I think they were having a party
or something.]

A party . . .

[And with all the smoke,
I couldn't see properly.]

I HANG ON HIS EVERY WORD

[I got turned around.]

Was it *my* party?

[I couldn't find my way out.]

And I couldn't get in.

[Then the roof collapsed.]

I shake my head.
No.
No!

It's too much of a coincidence . . .

It can't be!

IN MY DREAMS

In my nightmares,

there's always one person
who comes back.

I could have sworn
there was someone searching for me

in that quiet space
after the lightning

but before I woke up.

But I thought . . .

I thought it was
my dad, but now—

I STARTLE

as my curtain is wrenched open
and one of the nurses
lifts a finger to her lips.

“Shush!” she says, eyes wide
in the dim light.

“And you too, Vinny!” she calls.
“I will take that phone off you!”

She threatens before stalking back out.

THREE SINGLE LETTERS

sound from Vinny's phone.

[L.O.L.]

He must have put a period
after each one so it wouldn't
just say "lol."

"It's not funny," I tell him,
my voice smaller now.

I wish I could laugh.

[I'm sorry.]

What have I done?

[I'll have to wait until morning
to hear your story.]

What have I done?!

[Sweet dreams.]

"Sweet dreams," I reply,
though there's zero chance of that.

THE NEXT DAY

The doctors and nurses
do their morning rounds,

and we each lie there
as they check this and that.

Our vitals or whatever.

His burns
and mine.

I groan as they change my dressings.

They up my painkillers
and tell me to get more rest.

"I'm in bed, aren't I?"
I snap at the nurse.
Then apologize.

I'm so angry with everyone.
But most of all with myself.

WE FINALLY GET A BREAK

After the nurses have ceased
prodding and poking.

And I've had my first round of
physical therapy.

(It's only been a few days,
but they want me back on my feet
already.)

It's just us again.

VINNY ASKS

[You okay?]

No.
"I'm fine."

I swear I hear him audibly sigh.
[What's wrong?]

How can I . . . ?
How can I tell him everything?
Tell him the one thing
that could break this friendship?

I can't.
"I said I'm fine."

BUT OF COURSE I'M NOT

[Then why the long face?]

My gaze shoots over
to his curtained bay.

"What?" I ask, scanning
for gaps
for him to see me.

There are none.

The nurses make sure of it.

[L.O.L.] his phone voice says.

[Made you look.]

"No you didn't."

My cheeks burn.

"And you can't laugh out loud."

HE'S SILENT THEN

Did I take it too far?

"Vinny, I–"

[L.O.T.I.] his bot voice interrupts.

"L.O.T.I.?" I ask.

[Laugh on the inside.]

I can't help but smile.

"L.O.T.I."

I STARE OUT THE WINDOW

at the view he can't see.

He didn't deserve what happened to him.

He didn't deserve any of this,

and the fact I played
a part in it.

I suck in a breath,
but manage to hold back my tears.

The fact I played
such a huge role
in him being here,

in him being like this . . .

IT PAINS ME

more than the burns
that scorched my skin.

My exit wound is this.
My exit wound is him.

"I need to tell you something."

I wait for him to stop typing.

[I'm listening.]

"That house you ran in to?"

[yeah?]

I sniff back tears.
I have to do this.
I have to tell him.

FRIENDS DON'T KEEP SECRETS

"I think . . . that was my house."

[Huh?]

I wish I could hear his voice.
I wish I could see his face.

How am I supposed to know
what he's thinking,
how he's feeling,
when I can only talk to this curtain?

When he can only reply on his phone?

He can tell me he's laughing,
but I want to *hear* his laugh.

But after this . . .

WHAT IF HE CAN'T?

Even if he could.
What if he doesn't want to?

Not even on the inside?

What if.
What if.
What if.

TEARS TRACK MY CHEEKS

[Were you the girl I couldn't save?]

I turn away.

"Yes," I squeak
as my tears pour down.

"I had these . . . these friends
come over and . . ."

I try to swallow,
but I choke on the truth.

"They weren't even really my friends,
but I still said . . ."

I shake my head.
Why did I even do it?

"I said they could come over."

I WANTED THEM TO BE MY FRIENDS

"They asked to use my pool,
and I said they could."

[Okay. Then what?]

I sniff, and wipe my tears.

"Then the storm got bad.
Like really bad, and—"

I break into sobs.

"Eve locked me outside."

[What?]

I drop my face into my hands.
"I was locked outside,
and the thunder was so loud,
and the rain . . ."

HE STOPS TYPING

I carry on.

“They invited a bunch of people over.

It was like my whole school
was in my house.”

“And I was just out there.
Stuck.”

I’m shaking now.

“Then lightning hit the roof and—”

I couldn’t stop it.
I could only watch.

“Then . . .”

I gasp.

“Then, I guess it struck twice . . .
isn’t it not supposed to
strike twice?”

THERE'S A CLANG FROM BEHIND THE CURTAIN

Then a CRASH and the monitors
go berserk.

"Vinny?"

He's not typing.

"Vinny?!"

The curtain shifts,
and as footsteps race down
the corridor towards us,

beeps sound.
Alarms ring.

I can hear him,
getting closer.

He presses his hand
to the curtain between us.

"Vinny no! You'll hurt yourself!"

HIS PHONE FALLS TO THE FLOOR

And if I squint
I can see the tiny fracture in his screen.

"Help!" I yell,

but they're here already,
and there's shouting
and beeping,
and he can't talk.

And I can't see him.

Someone steps back,
and their heel meets his phone.

There's another loud CRACK
and it's not just splintered—

it's gone.

THEY SEDATE HIM

I guess.

Someone grabbed his broken phone.

Maybe they'll give him a notepad
or something?

A little whiteboard?

So he can still talk to *them*.

But it's not like
he can slide notes under the door,
under our curtain.

He's not allowed out of that bed.

If he tries again,
they'll restrain him.

"I'M SORRY, VINNY"

I tell him over and over.

"I'm so sorry."

I SPEND THE NIGHT IN SILENCE

The next morning passes
with a rush of nurses

wrapping and unwrapping me.

They test my balance
and assess my muscle atrophy.

My burns are healing,
and they tell me

I can go home soon.

But I don't want to leave.

And even when I do,
where will I go?

THE NEXT DAY

is my last day.

I'm leaving this place for good.

I swap my thin gown
for a black cotton dress
that Mom got in my size,
but it's swamping me now.

I stand up
and look down.

Mom grins.
"You've lost weight."

"Yeah," I deadpan. "I'm withering away."

She scowls. "Oh, don't be like that."

"Like what?" I ask.
I don't know why I'm so ready for a fight.

She crosses her arms.
"You look better, that's all."

I STAND MY GROUND

"I feel better."

I gesture to my arms and legs,
the needles and tubes all gone.

"Because my wounds are healing."

I meet her gaze.

"Not because I've lost a few pounds."

Mom sighs.

"I'll come back for you
when they call to say you're done,"
she says, like I'm a chicken
she's putting in the oven.

I KNOW HE'S STILL THERE

Because they talk to him,
his parents.

They're so kind.
They're here every single day.

And the nurses,
when they're doing their checks.

When they're feeding him,
and changing him,
bathing him.

When they're tending to the wounds
that he never would have had

had he not moved to our street,
had he never run into a fire

to save a stranger.

To save me.

MOM WILL COLLECT ME

at 5 o'clock.

I'm all packed and ready . . .
Well, I'm all packed.

"Vinny?" I try again.
"Vinny please. I'm going soon.

We're going to stay with
my aunt who has five cats,

which I'm allergic to.

But I guess I deserve that,
for being such a pushover.

For letting half the school
party at my house

in a thunderstorm."

I TELL HIM

"I wish I could go back.
If I could do it all again
I would tell them, *No*.

I wouldn't let them treat me like that,"
I speak louder,
praying he can hear.

I look over at my bag,
my pitiful amount of stuff.

I don't have anything to call my own.
Just the dress Mom bought for me.

I lost all my stuff,
all my clothes.

THE MOMENT I GAVE IN

I gave it all up.

"You've shown me what a real friend looks like."

I sigh.

What a stupid thing to say.

"Vinny. You're the only friend
I've ever had.

And the best friend
I could ever wish for.

And these last few days
should have been the worst time
of my life.

But they were some of the best.
Because of you.

Because of you,
I know what real friends

. . . sound like."

I LOOK OVER AT THE CURTAIN

which might as well be a wall of steel.

And though I have the strength
to reach out
and pull,

I can’t.

He doesn’t want to see me.
He doesn’t want to listen.
He doesn’t want to be my friend.

HE DOESN'T WANT ME

"Vinny. Please.
I'm so so sorry."

"Thought. You. Said . . .

You. Wouldn't.

. . . Apologize . . . Again?"

His voice is raspy.
His sentences broken.
Disjointed.

Rough like the guitars
from an old punk song.

Staggered like the offbeats
of a drum.

I TEAR BACK THE CURTAIN

"Vinny?"

It's really him.

He's not a blurry face,
or an obscured smile.

But flesh and blood
and bandages and burns.

The same lanky teen
who waved at me
Just a few days—

or was it a lifetime?

—ago.

Only now,
he's all beat up.

BROKEN

Burned.

"It's you," he rasps.

"Don't!" I cry. "You need to rest your voice.
I'm not worth it. Stop."

"I . . . hoped . . . it was . . . you."

I stare at him. "What?"

He smiles and rolls his eyes.

He's joking with me.

"I . . . just wanted . . . you to . . ."
He coughs and splutters.

"Vinny. Stop."

"I want . . . to . . . tell you . . . "

I LOOK AROUND

"Let me find you some paper,
a pencil. A pen—"

He reaches over,
and lays a gentle hand
on my loosely bandaged arm.

"You . . . were wearing . . .
a Frenzy State tee . . ."

"I guess, I—"

"Stop . . . guessing . . ."

"Okay."
Tears brim as I look down
at him in his hospital bed,

where he's been
this whole time.

"I wanted to . . . save the girl . . .
who . . . waved . . . at me."

BUT—

He holds my gaze
and I let him talk.

"I guess . . .

you . . . could say

it was . . . reckless . . .

what . . . I did . . ."

Tears stream down my face.
"You guess?"

I JUMP BACK

as the nurse storms in.

"Jordan!
Vinny?!"

The nurse
gapes at us both.

"I was just saying goodbye."

Her mouth twitches
as if she's going to scold us,
but instead she nods. "Okay then."

"Goodbye, Vinny."

"See . . . ya." He smiles.

THREE WEEKS LATER

I'm back in school.

Word quickly gets around.

Eve states, "I heard you nearly died."

I blink, shifting in my seat.

Then she leans in so close
her breath tickles my cheek.

"But like, I didn't
leave you out there
on *purpose*.

It was a *freak* accident."

She leans in closer still.
"You can't prove anything."

I STAND

Mr. Marshall clears his throat.
"Jordan? Is there a problem?"

"Actually . . ." My pulse quickens.

"Don't you dare—" Eve hisses.

I turn around, eyes wide.
Then I turn back.

Mr. Marshall frowns.
"Am I going to have to move you
away from your little friends?"

I shake my head.
"No. It's not that."

I can feel her watching me.
Eve's eyes like lasers
trained on the back of my head.

HIS FROWN DEEPENS

"It's just. I can't really see the board
from back here."

I glance behind me.

"And um . . ."

I take a breath.
Adjust my glasses.

"And . . .

they're not my friends."

HIS EYEBROWS RISE

"Well, okay then."
He gestures to one of the desks
in the front row.

"Did you want to sit here instead?"

I nod, then grab my stuff

and go.

I TAKE MY TIME

at the end of class,
to gather my things.

I no longer
feel the need
to charge out

like every second longer
that I stay
makes it harder to breathe.

Because I'm okay.
I'm . . . healing.

I'm free of my bandages,
and of Eve and her friends,
and of their hold over me.

OUTSIDE

They're waiting.

"What was that about?" Eve starts
before the door has even shut
behind me.

I shrug. "What was what?"

"What you said." She scowls.

I try not to look down
at my shoes,

which is what I usually do.

"That you're not my friends?"
I shrug. "Did you think we were?"

Eve glances at Jessie
and Sophia

while Lily remains slightly behind.

"It's just rude," Eve tells me.

SHE HUFFS

then stalks away,

Sophia and Jessie in tow.

But Lily hangs back.
"I thought it was kinda cool
actually . . ."

She glances around,
looking nervous.

"How you um . . . stood up for yourself
like that."

My eyebrows rise.
"You should watch out for Eve.
She's dangerous."

Lily nods.

"I think I
knew that,
deep down.
Thanks, Jordan."

She rushes off.

IT WAS LILY

She must've been the one
to tell the firefighters

I hadn't made it out.

AFTER SCHOOL

I get the bus.

My aunt lives miles away.

    I message Vinny,
    [HAPPY GOING HOME DAY!]

He replies,
[Thanks. What do you think?
Home today. Back gigging next week?]

    I laugh.
    [100%]
    [I'll run your merch stall!]

[Typical Jordan.]

    I shake my head, smiling.
    [What?]

[Such a groupie!]

I ROLL MY EYES

He's never gonna let that go,
is he?

I didn't have his number.

For a while,
I didn't even have a phone.

But the second I got one,
I looked up his band,

then I slid into his DMs.

[L.O.T.I.]

I refuse to indulge him by laughing
out loud.

[Talk tomorrow?]

I grin down at my phone.

IT'S NOT SO BAD

at my aunt's house.

Though there are six cats.
Not five.

I spend a lot of time sneezing.
And my eyes water
the second I walk through the door.

But, it's not like I can change
what happened,

and why we're here.

So, I guess I'll have to just
suck it up.

Our old house is gone.
And at least we've got a roof
over our heads.
(And that roof is not on fire!)

So I can't really complain.
And I don't.

IT'S ACTUALLY NICE SOMETIMES

Living with my aunt
means I'm never really alone.

Mom still works away a lot,
but instead of leaving me
to fend for myself,

I've got my aunt.
And a whole bunch of cats.

It's hard to feel lonely
when I've got all of that.

AND I'VE GOT VINNY TOO

Duh.

We talk all the time.
On the phone anyway.

But he's going home today,
which means he'll be starting
at my school some time
over the next few weeks.

(Once he's fully, **fully** recovered.)

Then I'll get to see him
nearly every day!

And maybe he'll get back to singing.
When he's ready.
When he's healed.

And if he does,
I'll be right there,
up against the barriers.

I'll have a front row seat.

IT'S WEIRD THOUGH

to think
he's going back to that house
across the street from
where my house used to be.

I don't know if I'll ever
go there.

I'm honestly not sure
I'll ever be able to face
our old street.

I still feel guilty
about it.

Even now.

It's something I have to live with
I guess.
I know.

But I survived,
which means I can live
with a lot of things.

And so, I will.

WANT TO KEEP READING?

If you liked this book, check out another book from West 44 Books:

GIRL CRUSH

BY C.H. WILLIAMS

ISBN: 9781978597693

CHECKPOINTS

There aren't any.

Where do we go in?

There are
no limits,
no boundaries,
no soldiers.

Every single house
is different.

Like, our house is blue.
Our house is BLUE!

Our street is like
a kiddie xylophone.

Each house is
a different color,
a different sound.

And ours
is blue.

MY ROOM IS BLUE, TOO

All the walls are painted
colors someone *chose*!

And Dad says
I can repaint it
any color I want!

I don't know where
to start.

I'm so used to white walls.
No. Not white.

Beige.
Cream.
Mag-no-li-a.

Dull. Dull. Dull.

BUT NOW . . .

The walls are my canvas.

I could even paint
the ceiling.

Imagine that!

A ceiling black as night
and full of stars

would be . . .

out of this world.

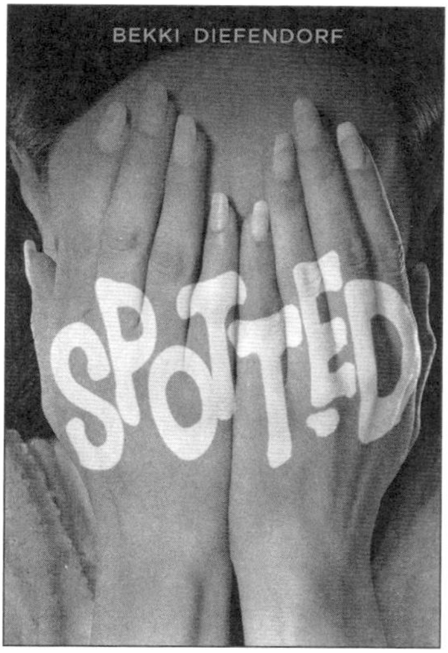

CHECK OUT MORE BOOKS AT:

www.west44books.com

WEST **44** BOOKS™

ABOUT THE AUTHOR

C.H. Williams is the author of the YA verse novels *Sign Me Up* and *Girl Crush*, and the MG verse novel *Kimmy Carson is Not Scared.* When she's not writing, she can be found hiking in the Welsh mountains with her golden retriever of a husband, and their wonderfully wild, nature-loving daughter.